A Career in...

Food Service

by Tom Streissguth

Illustrated with photographs
by Peter Ford

Capstone Press

MINNEAPOLIS

Printed in the United States of America.

Capstone Press • 2440 Fernbrook Lane • Minneapolis, MN 55447

Editorial Director   John Coughlan
Managing Editor   Tom Streissguth
Production Editor   James Stapleton
Book Design   Timothy Halldin

Library of Congress Cataloging-in-Publication Data

Streissguth, Thomas, 1958--
    A career in food service / Tom Streissguth
        p. cm.
    Includes bibliographical references and index.
    Summary: Provides brief descriptions of various jobs involved with preparing and serving food, including kitchen help, short-order cook, host or hostess, waiters and waitresses, and caterer.
    ISBN 1-56065-291-8
    1. Food service--Vocational guidance--Juvenile literature.
[1. Food service--Vocational guidance. 2. Occupations.]
I. Title.
    TX911.3.V62S77   1996
    647.95'023--dc20   95-11250
                                                                                    CIP
                                                                                    AC

Table of Contents

Chapter 1

Working in Food Service

Late afternoon is wearing into evening. The busy **rush hour** is past, but your job is just beginning. Before your customers arrive, you have a hundred jobs to do, and almost as many problems to solve.

As the head cook in a popular restaurant, you're a little bit like a movie star. Every night,

A cook carefully prepares a pastry shell for baking.

hundreds of people come to enjoy your talents. Newspapers and magazines feature articles about you. But your recipes are a secret—one

that makes you a valuable and honored employee.

Food service is a complicated and fascinating business. For managers, there are many important decisions to make every day. For cooks, there is the challenge of creating new and delicious recipes that will draw new customers. For **wait staff**, hosts, and others who serve the public, there is the pleasure of helping customers enjoy good food and interesting surroundings.

A career in food service is fast-paced and challenging. Workers in this field are learning every day, because tastes are always changing. Many food-service employees find that working in another field just isn't as much fun. They enjoy the bustle of a popular and successful restaurant. They can always train for new jobs in this fast-growing industry. With hard work, patience, and a bit of good luck, they may even taste success.

Chapter 2
Jobs in Food Service

Here are a few of the many different positions in the food-service field.

Fast-Food Worker

Fast-food restaurants employ people to prepare and serve simple, basic meals that can be cooked quickly. These businesses have **limited menus** that often include hamburgers, chicken, pizza, or many different kinds of fresh sandwiches.

Workers use small assembly lines to prepare menu items at a fast-food restaurant.

Customers don't like to wait long, so fast-food workers keep busy.

Some fast-food restaurants train their workers to perform all the jobs. In others, workers perform only one task. **Counter workers** must take orders from the customers, present the food when it's ready, and make change. Cooks prepare the food on a grill or in an oven, following a strict recipe and directions. Dining-room attendants keep the tables and floors clean and orderly.

Fast-food jobs are ideal for young students, because there are many openings and the hours are flexible. You can work part time, mornings, afternoons, or evenings. There are no education requirements. The restaurants will train their new employees or send them to a training school that will show them how to do the job.

Fast-food restaurant jobs are a good way to start out in the food-service industry. But if you are hired, you should be ready for a hectic job that takes a lot of energy. You also should be friendly, dress neatly, and work well with others.

Kitchen Help

A restaurant kitchen is a busy place. To prepare food for the public, the members of a kitchen staff must carry out many different tasks in a short amount of time. And during the busiest times, service to the customers can slow down if the cooks can't keep up with food orders.

To keep up, many restaurants hire full- or part-time kitchen helpers. Before the lunch or evening rush, kitchen helpers make soups, salads, sauces, and anything else that needs to be ready before cooks prepare the main courses. They peel vegetables, crack and mix eggs, and fix dessert portions. They also receive and stock food that arrives from outside **vendors**.

One of the most important jobs in restaurant work is keeping the kitchen clean. If the kitchen is dirty or disorganized, the restaurant can have a very serious problem. Public health departments make regular inspections, and inspectors can close a restaurant if it is unclean. And if a customer gets sick from a

Kitchen helpers may help cooks prepare simple items like eggs or pancakes.

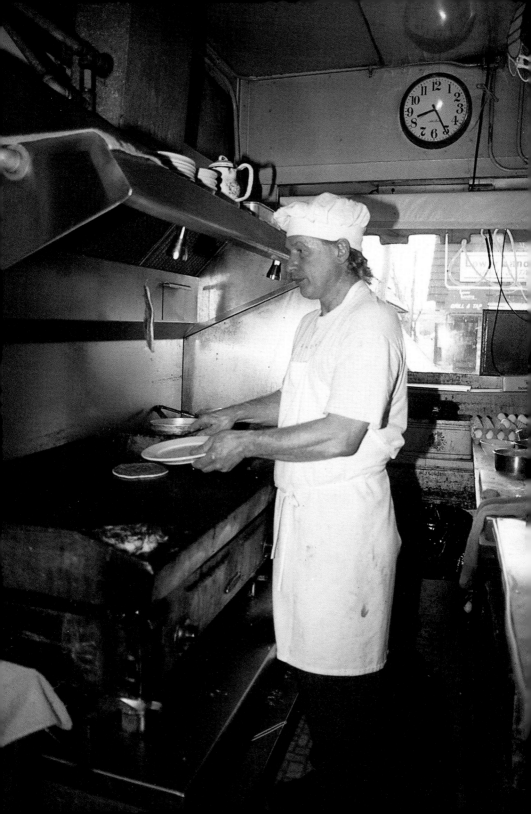

restaurant's unhealthy food, the news will keep other customers away for a long time.

To avoid this, kitchen helpers throughly clean cooking surfaces, such as stove tops and counters where food is prepared. They clean walls, floors, sinks, and dishwashers, and make sure unused food is always stored in a refrigerator.

Their work allows kitchen helpers to learn a lot about cooking food and managing a restaurant. There is little training, education, or experience required for the job. With time, it may lead to a better position.

Host/Hostess

The host is often the first person a guest meets in a restaurant. For that reason, men and women who work in this position must be friendly, neat, and ready to help.

Hosts and hostesses make **reservations** for customers who call before arriving. They arrange the customer seating and keep track of all the **reserved tables**. When customers arrive, the host or hostess must greet them, show them to their seats, and bring the menus.

Hosts and hostesses stay busy. If the restaurant does not have a **cashier**, they must settle the dinner checks and make change. Before leaving, they will count the money and make sure all the dinner checks have been paid.

A hostess sets tables before the dinner customers arrive.

Then they report the totals to the restaurant manager.

A high-school education is usually required for this job, and some restaurants demand previous experience. Some restaurants will train new employees. It is important to understand basic mathematics, such as addition and subtraction.

The salary of a host or hostess often depends on the restaurant. A more expensive restaurant will usually pay well for an experienced host. People in this occupation also have an opportunity to move into management. But unlike waiters and waitresses, they also must work a full-time schedule.

Short-Order Cook

The short-order cook prepares food, often very quickly. He or she must fix sandwiches, omelettes, steaks, and hot meals. Sometimes the restaurant is crowded, and all the customers are ordering at once. The cook has to keep track of many orders on the kitchen's stoves and counters. And he or she must let the servers know when the food is ready.

Many times, customers order their food prepared a special way. The cook must know how to do eggs **over easy**, or a steak **medium well**. If a dish cooks too long on the stove, or if the customer isn't satisfied for some reason, the cook will have to start all over again.

A short-order cook chats with customers during a break.

Restaurant cooks must work hard to get orders done and out to the customer quickly.

Before the rush, the short-order cook prepares food. He or she slices potatoes, lettuce, tomatoes and carrots. Soups and salads must be made, and meats must be cut in the right portions for sandwiches.

There are many skills a short-order cook should have. He or she must be skillful–and careful–with sharp **utensils**, hot stoves, and heavy food containers. The cook must handle pressure, and must work well with waiters and waitresses. Like many other restaurant jobs, the position of short-order cook demands a lot of teamwork.

Previous experience working in a restaurant kitchen is good preparation for this job. In addition, many vocational schools offer courses in restaurant cooking.

The skilled short-order cook can go on to become a chef in a better restaurant. Ambitious short-order cooks may decide to open a new restaurant on their own.

Waiter/Waitress

The restaurant waiter or waitress holds a very important job–representing the restaurant to the customer. Many customers make their choice of restaurant based on service. As a result, the wait staff can be a big part of a restaurant's success or failure.

Waiters and waitresses must know the menu and the style of cooking that the restaurant offers. While working, they must also be able to handle stressful situations and difficult customers.

For each shift, the restaurant manager assigns a **station** to each waiter. Each station includes several tables. The waiter for that station is responsible for keeping track of all the orders at each table.

After customers are seated, the waiter may give menus, water, and free **appetizers** to the customers. He or she then explains the menu selections and describes any special dinners the restaurant is offering. When customers are ready, the waiter takes their orders, making sure to note if the customer wants food prepared a special way.

The waiter passes orders to the kitchen and then brings the food to the customer when the meal is ready. It is very important to bring the food as quickly as possible and to remember what each customer ordered.

At the end of the meal, the waiter serves desserts and coffee, and then brings the bill to

A waitress gives instructions to the cook.

the table. If the customer wishes to pay
immediately, the waiter must accept checks or
cash, or prepare a credit-card **receipt**.

Patience, courtesy, neatness, and **stamina**
are all important to a waiter or waitress. Good
service usually brings good **tips,** which are the
largest part of the waiter's pay. In expensive
restaurants, the tips are higher, but the job can
be harder. In some of these businesses, waiters

must be familiar with foreign terms and with unusual dishes that the restaurant may be offering.

Cook/Chef

The restaurant cook is mainly responsible for selecting items that will appear on the menu and preparing them. The cook also decides how the food will be prepared, what ingredients

While under pressure, cooks have to handle foods carefully and follow recipes exactly.

each dish will contain, and how large the portions will be.

Cooks may decide that a dish is no longer interesting or popular, and drop it from the menu. The cook also may create new dishes, using his or her imagination and skills. Some cooks have become famous for a single dish. A single menu item that customers enjoy may be responsible for a restaurant's success.

Baking desserts calls for precise timing.

Laying out portions on the plate is a demanding skill in itself. Good presentation of meals is an important part of a cook's success.

There are many places besides restaurants that hire cooks. Hotel kitchens employ cooks to prepare food for their guests. Many companies hire cooks for their own cafeterias, where employees can enjoy freshly prepared food. Schools, military bases, private clubs, and hospitals also employ cooks.

There are many different kinds of specialized cooking jobs. Pastry cooks prepare bread, rolls, pastries, and cakes for dessert menus. Fry cooks and vegetable cooks prepare only certain menu items. There are also salad cooks, soup cooks, and sauce cooks.

Many cooks start in one of these specialized positions, then work their way up to head cook. They learn on the job, or take courses in cooking at **vocational school**. Most restaurants require new cooks to have at least a high-school **diploma**.

Cooks should love their work, because it is physically demanding. They must lift heavy pots and pans, stand for hours at a time, and work over hot stoves. They also must work well with others and be ready to manage the people working for them in the kitchen.

Caterer

Most people enjoy eating at a restaurant. But sometimes they need restaurant food and

service for a special occasion at their home or business. They will place an order to a professional caterer.

The caterer works from a store, or from his or her own kitchen. He or she prepares food that customers order for special occasions.

Caterers often have to prepare many small portions for their clients.

These include parties, meetings, and other social gatherings. Some caterers also provide special tableware, furniture, or decorations for the event.

Caterers must know how to prepare many different kinds of breads, salads, dinners, and desserts. They have a long menu of available foods for the customer to choose from. This menu changes as customers stop ordering certain items and as new foods become popular.

Caterers must often work under pressure. All the food must be ready and delivered on time. It takes much planning and hard work to meet customer demands during holidays or in the busy summer season.

Many caterers specialize in a certain kind of food, such as French, Mexican, or Chinese. Others are ready to prepare just about anything that people throwing parties may demand.

Caterers must understand how to run a business as well as how to prepare food. They have to keep track of accounts, buy food and supplies, and record their income and expenses. They also should be good at **marketing**–the job of promoting a business to customers. There is a lot of competition in the field, so caterers must constantly work to do their job a little better.

Bartender

Bartenders prepare beverages–both alcoholic and non-alcoholic–for customers. A bartender may work in a restaurant, in a bar with a limited menu, or in a bar that serves only drinks. He or she is responsible for mixing drinks, stocking supplies, and keeping the bar area clean. In some restaurants, the bartender helps the wait staff prepare the dining room for customers.

Most customers want to relax and talk while visiting the bartender's workplace.

Bartenders must know how to prepare many different kinds of drinks. They must dress neatly. They should also enjoy working late hours and talking with their customers. Restaurants require them to know the laws about serving alcoholic beverages. In many restaurants, new bartenders must be at least 25 years old.

Bartenders may learn on the job, or they may train at a bartending or vocational school. After their first job, they may move on to more expensive restaurants or bars, where they may earn more in salary and tips.

There are many other jobs in the food-service industry, a business that has been through many changes. In the future, new kinds of eating establishments may open to the public, demanding different knowledge and skills. But the basic task of a food-service worker–to prepare and serve good food to the public–will always be important.

Chapter 3
Getting Ready

Here are some useful steps that can help you get ready for a career in the food-service field.

Read. Study job guides that focus on restaurant work. They will list qualifications and training necessary for each job, as well as average salaries offered. They may also give you an idea of regions where food-service work will be readily available.

Cook. Try preparing simple dishes at home. Learn how certain sauces and spices change the flavor of salads, soups, and main courses. Listen carefully to the opinions of people who try your food. Ask them what they like and dislike about it. Keep a notebook of your discoveries.

Talk. Speak with people already working in the food-service industry. Ask them how they started, and what their future plans are. Ask to visit their workplace during slow hours.

Volunteer. Call a local charity and offer to help prepare or serve food for the needy.

Go online. Use an online computer service to strike up conversations with cooks or other food-service professionals.

Study. Take courses in cooking or restaurant management at a vocational or technical school. Read books on the business of restaurant management.

There are more than 5 million people working in the food-service industry today. It's a wide-open field, with new jobs available every day. Some day, you may find one suited to your ambition and ability.

Glossary

appetizers–small menu items or snacks served before the main course

cashier–a worker who accepts payment from customers for their meals

counter worker–a worker who takes food orders at a counter. Counter workers may also handle payment and prepare drinks and some menu items.

diploma–a certificate received after finishing a course of study

limited menu–a short list of menu items available to restaurant customers. Many restaurants, especially fast-food businesses, offer only limited menus.

medium well–to prepare meat so that it is cooked throughout

over easy–to prepare eggs by turning them once on the grill and then serving them

receipt–a paper showing money paid for food or service

reservations–orders to hold a table open for customers who will arrive later

reserved tables–tables that are being held for customers holding reservations

rush hour–the busiest hours of operation, usually lunch and dinner times

stamina–the ability to perform physical work for a long period of time

station–a set of tables at which a waiter or waitress is responsible for service

tips–money offered to a worker for good service

utensils–kitchen tools, such as knives, forks, and spoons, that are used to prepare food

vendors–businesses who sell services or goods to other businesses

vocational school–a institute that trains students for jobs

wait staff–the group of restaurant workers who serve food to the customers

To Learn More

Ancona, George. *And What Do You Do? A Book about People and Their Work.* New York: Dutton, 1976.

Cavallaro, Ann. *Careers in Food Service.* New York: Elsevier/Nelson Books, 1981.

Primm, E. Russell, Editor-in-Chief. *Career Discovery Encyclopedia.* Chicago: Ferguson Publishing Company, 1990.

Snelling, Robert O. *Jobs!* New York: Simon and Schuster, 1989.

Tomchek, Ann Heinrichs. *I Can Be a Chef.* Chicago: Childrens Press, 1985.

Some Useful Addresses

American Culinary Federation
P.O. Box 3466
St. Augustine, FL   32085

American Hotel and Motel Association
1201 New York Avenue NW
Washington DC 20005

**Council on Hotel, Restaurant and
  Institutional Education**
1200 17th St. NW
Washington DC 20036

National Restaurant Association
1200 17th St, NW
Washington DC 20036

Index

For special occasions, caterers offer a wide selection of desserts to their customers.

46